OH BEANS!
St★rring Boston Bean

BY ELLEN WEISS • ILLUSTRATED BY SUSAN T. HALL

Troll Associates

Boston Bean was the richest bean in town. Anything you can think of, Boston Bean had two.

"Ah-HA!" you might yell. "I'll bet he didn't have gold-plated Ping-Pong paddles!"

Well, as a matter of fact, he did.

"Well, then," you might say, "he probably didn't have a silver toothbrush."

Wrong again. In fact, he had four. Just in case company came over. But—he never had company. You see, there was one thing Boston Bean didn't have.

Friends.

Boston Bean had everything money could buy. Some beans thought that with all those things, Boston Bean was the happiest bean in town.

But they were wrong.

One summer day, Boston Bean woke up early. "Another beautiful day," he said to himself, "and nobody to share it with. Boston, old bean, it's time to make some friends."

So off he went to town.

First, he passed the Beantown ball field and saw Lima Bean and String Bean playing ball. They were laughing and running and getting dirty. Boston Bean wanted to join in, but he didn't know how to ask.

Next, Boston Bean passed Vanilla Bean's house.

She was serving some freshly baked cookies to Green Bean.

Boston Bean wished he could taste the cookies, but he was too shy to ask.

Boston Bean sat down on the curb, feeling very sad. "I'd give everything I own to have some friends," he said to himself.

That gave him an idea! "Maybe I can get friends the same way I get everything else—I'll buy them!"

Along came slippery old Wax Bean, twirling his mustache. Wax Bean was not one of the nicer beans in Beantown. In fact, he was a real rat, and greedy, too, if you want to know the truth. "Why so glum, chum?" said Wax Bean.

"I don't have any friends," Boston Bean sighed. "If I gave you a dollar, would you be my friend?"

"Why, certainly," said Wax Bean. "And if you gave me three dollars, I'd be your *very* good friend."

"That's wonderful!" said Boston Bean.

"It sure is," agreed Wax Bean. "See you later, *friend*!" And off he went, counting his money.

Along came Mean Bean, another rotten bean.

"Hi," said Boston Bean, feeling more sure of himself. "Would you be my friend? I'll give you three dollars."

"Sure," said Mean Bean. If Boston Bean was going to act like a beanbrain, he wouldn't mind taking advantage of him.

Boston Bean smiled. "Hey, I guess this is how everybeany makes friends," he said to himself. When Vanilla Bean came along, he was ready for her.

"Hi," he said. "If I gave you three dollars, would you be my friend?"

Vanilla Bean just stared. She was a whole different kettle of beans from Boston Bean's first two "friends."

"Okay, five dollars," Boston Bean offered.

Vanilla Bean turned white. "What kind of bean do you think I am?" she said. Then she fled down the street.

String Bean and Lima Bean came by next, out of breath and laughing.

"Er—hello," said Boston Bean, shuffling his feet. "If I gave you ten dollars each, would you be my friends?"

"WHAT?" said String Bean. "You want to *pay* us to be your friends?"

"You must be kidding," said Lima Bean.

And they walked off, shaking their heads.

Boston Bean sat on the curb, staring at his feet. He was feeling more confused than ever. What could have gone wrong? Why were people suddenly running away from him?

All of a sudden, two tiny feet appeared before his. Boston Bean looked up, to see Bean Sprout—the tiniest bean in town.

"Will you play beanball with me?" squeaked Bean Sprout. "Will you be my friend?"

"How much will it cost?" asked Boston Bean.

"Nothing, silly," said Bean Sprout. "I just want somebody who has time to play with me. Will you?"

"Sure!" said Boston Bean, jumping up. "You bet! All right!"

So, Boston Bean and Bean Sprout went down to the ball field and started playing beanball. They laughed and giggled and ran up and down the field.

"Hey, that looks like fun," called Jumping Bean, who was passing by. "Can I play, too?"

"Sure!" said Boston Bean. "Here's the ball!"

Then Lima Bean and String Bean came back and decided to join in the fun.

Soon, just about everybody in Beantown was playing beanball.

"Here it comes!" Bean Sprout threw the ball, Boston Bean caught it, and everybody landed in a big pile-up.

"You're tickling me, Vanilla Bean!" laughed Boston Bean. She tickled him some more.

And then he realized: he was right at the bottom of a pile of—friends! *Real* friends, not fake ones like Wax Bean and Mean Bean. And *making* friends was much more fun than *buying* them!

Boston Bean was very happy. "Bean a friend," he said, tickling Vanilla Bean back, "is much better than anything money can buy!"